To Samrawit,
with love and laughter,
Bubbe
-S.A.

For the West Linn Public
Library librarians and all the
kids, dogs, *and* chickens that
enjoy the library
-M.F.

Dial Books for Young Readers | Penguin Young Readers Group
An imprint of Penguin Random House LLC | 375 Hudson Street, New York, NY 10014

Copyright © 2016 by Sandy Asher. Illustrations copyright © 2016 by Mark Fearing.

Library of Congress Cataloging-in-Publication Data
Names: Asher, Sandy. | Fearing, Mark, illustrator. Title: Chicken story time / by Sandy Asher ; pictures by Mark Fearing.
Description: New York, New York : Dial Books for Young Readers, an imprint of Penguin Group (USA), [2016]
Summary: Storytime in the library becomes increasingly chaotic as first one chicken then a whole flock joins in and the librarian must come up with a creative solution so that everyone can enjoy the story.
Identifiers: LCCN 2014048400 | ISBN 9780803739444 (hardcover)
Subjects: | CYAC: Chickens—Fiction. | Books and reading—Fiction. | Librarians—Fiction. | Humorous stories.
Classification: LCC PZ7.A816 Ch 2016 | DDC [E]—dc23 LC record available at http://lccn.loc.gov/2014048400

Printed in China.

10 9 8 7 6 5 4 3 2

Design by Jennifer Kelly | Text set in Burbank
The illustrations in this book were created using traditional and digital tools.

CHICKEN STORY TIME

Sandy Asher

ILLUSTRATED BY
Mark Fearing

Dial Books for Young Readers

Story time at the library.

One librarian. One story. Children.

And a chicken.

The children like the chicken.

The chicken likes the children.

"Let's begin," says the librarian.

Everyone loves story time.

One week later.
Story time at the library.

One librarian.

One story.

More children.

More chickens.

The children like the chickens.
The chickens like the children.
"Please be seated," says the librarian.

Everyone loves story time.

One week later.
Story time at the library.

One librarian. One story.

Many children.

Many chickens.

The children laugh.

The chickens cluck.

CLUCK CLUCK CLUCK!

CLUCK CLUCK CLUCK!

"Settle down now," says the librarian.
No one can hear her.

CLUCK!

BAWWWK CLUCK!

Children and chickens everywhere, but only one librarian.

"What are we to do?" she says.

CLUCK! CLUCK CLUCK CLUCK!

Story time at the library.

Lots of children.
Flocks of chickens.

Shelves and shelves of stories.

The children like the chickens.

The chickens like the children.

Everyone loves story time...

...especially the librarian.